Festival of the Damned

A Folk Horror Novella

Newton Webb

Steel Crown Productions

Contents

Chapter One

1st May, 2013, Huddersford, Kent

The coach pulled into Huddersford station. As it came to an abrupt stop and the brakes screeched, Faith stirred in Elsie's lap. Stroking her hair, Elsie smiled at the mousey little girl. 'Wake up, sleepy head, we've arrived.'

Elsie watched as Faith looked around her and out of the coach windows. She scrunched her eyes and rubbed the sleep out of them. The town was milling with people on their way to work. They could hear the dense chatter of a town small enough for people to recognise their neighbours but big enough to fill a depot with commuters.

'Come along, poppet.' She gestured to the exit. Shouldering her backpack, she guided Faith up and out of her seat. The two of them joined the queue of people as they made their way down the cramped gangway.

A tall, burly boy in his late teens was waiting by the luggage bags. He leaned back against the coach and grinned when he saw Elsie. 'Name's Blake. Now, tell me, what's a beautiful girl like you doing in a shithole like this?'

Elsie winced at the boy's clumsy chat-up line as she shuffled along with the other disembarking passengers towards the luggage hold. She looked up at him nervously and smiled. 'Work, how about you?'

He looked up as they threw his bag out of the luggage area and leant down to grab it, slinging it over his shoulder. His muscular arms bulged under its weight. Elsie's much smaller bag appeared and she gripped it, pulling it clear with effort.

'I got a shitty gig dressing up like a bird for a country fair.' He grinned. 'They called it an acting job. I almost dismissed it because I've never done acting in my life. But a job's a job. What's your name and your—' he squinted at Faith '—sister's name?'

'Elsie, this is—'

'My name's Faith,' her sister chipped in, reaching out her hand confidently. Blake shook it politely. 'My sister's doing the same thing. She is dressing up as a rabbit. I am going to do it too, but I had to bring my own costume.' Faith rummaged around in Elsie's backpack and found a pair of bunny ears to stick on her head.

'Hey, my battery charger's missing.' A gangly looking teen was going through his bag. Panic gripped Elsie. She had only one real possession of value. Quickly opening up her bag, she rummaged around with a sense of encroaching dread.

Elsie stopped, biting her bottom lip to hold back the tears. It was gone. She had also been robbed.

'Are you okay?' Blake asked.

Faith came over and held her hand. Elsie shook her head. 'Not really, it's gone. The only photo I have of my mother and me, before she... There isn't another copy. I should have sold the stupid silver frame and put it in something cheaper.' Grief wracked her. *Idiot. You stupid idiot.* 'It was all I had left of her.'

Faith and Elsie had been for a day out to Brighton with her. They'd taken the photo on the pier. She'd never see her mother again.

'I'm sorry, girl.' Blake went in for a hug. Elsie pushed him away, eyes wide with horror. 'Whoa, sorry, I misjudged that situation.'

Elsie gasped. 'No, it is, no, I just don't like to be touched. I'm sorry. Thank you for your kindness.'

The other victim had marched up to the coach driver and was busy haranguing him. Elsie looked at Blake. 'I'm sorry, please excuse me,' she said, before joining him.

The driver, a haggard, middle-aged man with a balding pate, was shrugging. 'Nothing I can do, mate. Call this number. It's lost property. They'll help you.'

'Hey, are you guys going to this festival thing? I overheard you chatting.' Elsie turned to see a short girl with her black hair cut into a bob, the tips dyed purple. 'I mean, total drag, but it's easy money, right? I'm... 'The Fox', sometimes called Zoe.' She mimicked a sexy growl.

'I'm Elsie, and I'm 'The Hare'.' Elsie smiled wanly. The theft had torpedoed her appetite for social interaction.

'I'm Blake, and I'm 'The Pheasant'.' Holding out his hand, Blake shook her hand with enthusiasm.

'Sorry, I have to call this number. Come on, Faith.'

Faith shook her head. 'I'm staying with these two.'

Elsie grabbed her arm. 'The hell you are. You need to stick with me.'

As she dragged Faith away with her, she saw Zoe looking at her with a bemused expression on her face.

'Why couldn't I stay with them?' Faith asked.

Elsie gave her a hug, then looked deep into her eyes. 'It's just us now. We have to stick together. There is nobody else for us. Do you understand?'

'I know, I just wish things were like they were before.' Faith's lip trembled. 'I miss my room.'

'We can't go back, Faith, you know that.' Elsie stroked her hair. 'Not any more.'

Faith nodded and Elsie called lost property. It took fifteen minutes of queueing to get to a human voice and another five to help the bored sounding operator fill out their form. They left her with absolutely no confidence that they would find it.

With a sunken feeling in her chest, she and Faith rejoined the other actors who were waiting expectantly.

As she strode towards them, she loaded up the route on her phone. 'It's a three-mile walk to the village from here.' Elsie saw that it was all uphill and muttered a quiet curse.

Blake patted her on the shoulder. 'I'll get us a taxi, no worries.'

Elsie flinched. 'We don't have any money.'

'Ha.' Blake reached down and grabbed her luggage. 'Don't you worry, I get a bit of scratch from my gran. I can pay. It's only up the hill.'

'Any room for a Fox in that taxi?' The newcomer slid her hand up Blake's muscular arm.

Blake winked. 'Always room for a Fox, girlio.'

'I'll pay half.' Blake turned, annoyed to see another male. It was the gangly teen with the missing phone. 'I'm playing the Badger. Name's Calvin, ain't it.'

'Why are you the Badger? You're half my size. I'll tell you what mate, you let me be the Badger and I'll let you join our taxi.' Blake pointed with Elsie's bag to a taxi rank on the other side of the coach station.

'Whatever, I don't mind, I'm just doing this for the money. I'll play any animal, really. I don't know if we get to--'

'--Perfect, then it's settled. *I'm* the Badger and *you* are the Pheasant.'

Zoe followed him as Blake marched towards the taxis. 'And a big, strong badger you are too.'

Grimacing at the transparent flirtation, Elsie followed her luggage as Blake carried it for them.

'Come on, Elsie,' Faith said, tugging her towards the waiting cars. Elsie surrendered to the inevitable and followed them as they assembled around a six-seater minivan.

The minivan drove them up a winding road to the top of the hill, where scattered houses gave way to a dense cluster of four-bed dwellings built in the last century. Miniature gardens, flawlessly manicured, were paired with well-maintained brick homes. Dogs watched from the gates and curtains twitched as the locals watched vigilantly.

'Look at the forest!' Calvin had his face pressed up against the window. They peered out. Sure enough, acres upon acres of fruit trees stretched into the distance down the hill from the village.

Faith watched, eyes wide. She had spent her life in Elephant and Castle. The countryside was new to her and this... this was a whole lot of nature.

'Well, I can't wait to get out of this hell hole and back to civilisation.' Zoe pulled out a vanity mirror and adjusted her makeup.

Relaxing between Zoe and Elsie, Blake leaned back. 'I don't mind it. Experiencing a bit of the outdoors could be fun.'

'And I love that.' Zoe leaned into him. He instinctively put his arm around her. Elsie's eyes rolled.

The taxi dropped them off at the village pub where they were to meet their contact Geoff, who would brief them on their gig at the Festival. As they walked into the pub, they saw the friendly, curious smiles of the local villagers with their tankards of cider.Wooden picnic tables were scattered across a grassy garden. Picking one as far away from the locals as possible, they all congregated. A group of kids chased each other around a giant bush on one side of the pub garden. Faith watched them enviously, but settled down next to Elsie.

Zoe shivered at the cold air and nestled into Blake for warmth.

'Well, that didn't take long,' Calvin snarked.

Blake grinned amiably while Zoe narrowed her eyes at the remark.

'Look at you.' A rotund man with tortoiseshell rimmed glasses and a vibrant waistcoat bounced towards them. 'What a marvellous bunch of beautiful thespians we have here, brimming with vim and vigour.' Circling the table, his twinkling eyes graced them with a welcoming smile. 'Oh, I used to tread the boards myself in my youth in the village hall. How I remember the acrid scent of the greasepaint, the heat of the lights and the ghastly lack of pockets.'

'Sorry, I'm Elsie. Who are you?' She suspected the answer, but it was always better to check.

'I'm sorry! Oh, gracious me. I'm Geoff.' Geoff laughed. 'What a buffoon! I apologise profoundly. You must have thought I was lampooning you like an absolute cad. I tell you what, how about I get you all some lovely freshly squeezed lemonade and brief you about your upcoming performance?'

Blake pointed to the locals nearby. 'Actually, I think I'd rather have a cider. I'm nineteen, not nine.'

Geoff preened, tucking his thumbs into his waistcoat. 'But of course! Our cider is the best in Britain. Award-winning. That is why you are here! In its divine magnificence, the woods call for a festival in its honour and if successful, it rewards us all with fifty years of hearty harvests.' Geoff took a moment to drink in the wisdom of his own words before seeming to remember them. 'Of course, a pint for the young sir. Anyone else?'

A chorus of hands shot up, including Faith, who had her hand dragged down by Elsie. Geoff noticed her as if for the first time.

A frown crossed his face as he leaned in. 'And who is this? A fifth actor? Most irregular.'

'I need to keep an eye on her. She'll stay in the dressing rooms,' Elsie said.

Pulling out a pair of bunny ears, Faith put them on. 'I'm a bunny.'

Geoff roared with laughter, 'A leveret! Of course.'

'No, I'm a bunny. I was most clear.' Faith regarded the man with a disgruntled look. Elsie gently rested her hand on Faith's arm.

'Of course, a baby hare. I'm just sorry that we don't have a role for you on the stage. 'This festival'–he looked around, waving his arm expansively at the orchard–'is over a thousand years old. Every fifty years, we put on the festival to renew our vows to Cernunnos.'

The teens looked at him blankly, except for Zoe, who was snuggling deep into Blake's chest.

'Care Snu Nose?' Faith attempted.

'Care-Nu-Nos! The Horned God, the lord of fertility. He was called Pan by the Greeks and Bacchus by the Romans. He ensures a plentiful harvest and healthy herds.' Looking around with fake discretion, he whispered, 'He is also the god of libations and other more adult pursuits,' Geoff chuckled. 'But you should wait a few years until you find out about those pleasures.'

'Gross!' Elsie muttered.

'Now then, pints of cider for the men and halves for the ladies.' Geoff turned to go.

'I'll have a whole pint, please,' Elsie said.

'And me,' Zoe chipped in.

Geoff gave a nervous chuckle. 'Oh, of course, the modern generation. What a marvel. It is quite impossible to fathom.'

As he walked away, Zoe looked up from where she had attached herself limpet-like to Blake. 'So that just happened.'

'Yep, we've officially been patronised.' Elsie shrugged. 'But we are getting paid.'

'I don't like him. He's weird.' Faith wriggled on her seat, her legs dangling down. 'I wanted to be part of the festival.'

Smiling at Faith, Zoe returned her attention to Blake.

Calvin pointed at the two of them. 'So, that, this, bit fast innit.'

'What do you mean?' Blake said, his heavy brow furrowed.

Calvin laughed bitterly. 'What do I mean? You met five minutes ago and now you are what? Dating?'

'Is the little bird jealous?' Zoe gave a wicked smile, her eyes gleaming.

'She's just cold.' Blake put his arm around Zoe and gave her a warm hug.

'Freezing.' Zoe slid a hand up Blake's thigh, causing him to look embarrassed.

Elsie pulled her phone out of her pocket and was googling Cernunnos. 'Oh my god, it turns out, Cernunnos *is* a thing. That is disgusting. They used to host orgies in his name. It's where the Christian harvest festival came from.'

'Christian orgies?' Zoe gagged. 'Sandal sex. I bet they all do it whilst wearing socks and cardigans. I hope they don't do that tonight. Imagine Geoff's fat, liver-spotted belly sashaying around.'

'Child present,' Elsie warned.

Faith giggled.

'How did the church go from orgies to sticking candles in oranges?' Zoe said.

'That is Christingle. Harvest Festival is the one where you take packets of instant noodles and tins of soup to church,' Blake said. When the others looked at him, he shrugged, embarrassed. 'I used to go with my gran to church on Sundays to make sure she got there okay.'

Geoff chose that moment to appear with a tray of cider tankards and crisps. 'I have ordered some chips for you to fatten my budding thespians up for the festival.'

He handed out four sheets of laminated cards. 'These are your lines. I numbered them for the order you'll speak in. The high priest will say his lines, then...' Geoff paused expectantly.

Elsie raised her hand, 'I say mine.'

'Very good and so forth. Then we get a closing statement from the 'high priest', who will end it with...' Geoff braced himself, 'Release the hounds.' He waved theatrically and boomed. 'That's my favourite part. Then you must run through the woods back to the pub wearing your masks the whole way. After a five-minute head start, you'll be chased by a chosen group of villagers wearing hound masks. If they touch you, you just fall to the ground with a shriek. They'll tie your hands with a hemp rope and lead you back to the festival where the high priest will give a reading.'

'What happens if we make it back to the pub?' Elsie asked.

'Well, your rooms are here so you'll get a good night's sleep. But you'll also get a reward.' Geoff winked, his jowls jiggling from the movement. '*Two hundred and fifty* pounds. I'll be waiting back here with four envelopes and I truly hope you all make it back. This is a wonderful opportunity to have a starring role in a once a century cultural event. I'm immensely jealous of you all.'

Elsie smiled politely. 'And our payment?'

'Oh, good lord, yes. Of course, of course. You'll be paid in full in the morning. You can order a taxi to the coach station using the pub landline. Now, do you have any bags to drop off? We have reserved rooms for you here.'

They looked at their luggage and affirmed.

'Then follow me, my marvellous herd, and let's get you settled.' Geoff took them upstairs and doled out the room keys, apologising that there was only one bed for Elsie and Faith.

Elsie, Faith and Calvin regrouped around the picnic table. Several plates of thick cut chips arrived, steaming.

'Shouldn't we wait...' Faith started.

'No,' Elsie and Calvin said immediately in unison. 'I think the other two are busy,' Elsie said, blowing on a chip to cool it down.

Faith giggled.

'They weren't joking.' Calvin had taken a long slurp of cider. 'This is delicious!'

Picking up a tankard and taking a sip. Elsie's eyes widened. 'This *is* delicious.'

'Let me, let me!' Faith reached out.

'Absolutely not. You are far too young.' Elsie took another sup. 'And this is far too delicious to share.'

'But Elsie!' pleaded Faith.

'No buts,' Elsie said sternly.

'Where was that rule earlier?' Zoe said, stalking towards them, lips pursed and glowing from ear to ear.

Blake followed behind her, smiling amiably. 'Alright, everyone?'

'That didn't take long,' muttered Calvin. He looked at his cider sourly.

Settling down, Blake looked at the half-empty plates of chips. 'Thanks for waiting.'

'Well, we didn't know if you'd be joining us,' Elsie said, looking around for a distraction. She lifted up her tankard. 'Have you tried the cider?'

Blake took a gulp. His eyes closed and he murmured with contentment. He took another sip before he could reopen them. 'Fuck me, this is good.'

Zoe smirked. 'I bet I have tasted something better.' Elsie chose to ignore her. When she realised nobody was paying her any attention, Zoe glowered, gulping down the cider with a sour expression.

'No wonder they keep winning best in Britain. This is great.' Blake enthused. He had already finished his pint.

'Anyone want another?' Blake raised his empty tankard.

Looking at her half-full tankard, Elsie shrugged. 'Yes, please.'

'I'll get them.' Calvin offered.

'It's alright, I already offered, mate.' Blake grinned, starting to rise.

'No, I said I'll get them.' Calvin spluttered. His face was red and angry. 'I want to buy them.'

'Jesus! Alright, mate. Whatever, I was just being nice.' Blake sat back down, embarrassed. 'I didn't mean to cause upset.'

'It's fine.' Calvin rose, leaving his barely touched cider on the table as he went to get a round.

Waiting until he was inside, Zoe looked at the others. 'What a little psycho.'

'What was all that about?' Elsie asked. Blake shrugged.

They sat awkwardly until Calvin returned and handed each of them a tankard of cider.

Taking another sip of her cider, Elsie rose. 'This cider is going right through me. Did anyone notice where the toilets are?'

'Just head straight to the left. They are by the fireplace.' Blake said.

Elsie walked inside. The pub was comfy. Stone walls were covered with old paintings and countryside knick-knacks, horseshoes, awards for their cider, mounted animal heads, and even an ornate crossbow above the bar. The warm sound of friendly banter echoed around the walls. As she walked past a subdued fire, the scent of cider, bleach and smoke filled her nostrils.

She found the toilet quickly enough, sitting down and closing her eyes. This is it. This is the day life begins anew for her and Faith.

Elsie emerged from the pub to hear loud swearing. Quickening her pace, she reached the exit and saw Calvin standing, pointing and yelling at Faith who, in contrast, was laughing at him.

'You stupid bitch,' Calvin vented. Calvin's finger was pointing like the barrel of a gun. Blake had his palm against Calvin's chest, blocking him from Faith.

Elsie sped up. 'What is going on?' Calvin turned around, shocked. 'Why are you swearing at my sister? She is only fourteen. What did she do?'

'*She* drank your cider. I was defending you,' Calvin protested.

'What the fuck is it to you? She is my sister. That was my cider. She is my responsibility.' Elsie was close to the table now and showed no sign of slowing down. Anger coursed through her voice.

Calvin blathered something unintelligible that she assumed was his pathetic attempt at an apology.

'What's going on here?' A group of men from a neighbouring table had risen. 'Everyone is trying to have a nice quiet pint here.'

Blake imposed his bulk between Elsie and Calvin, gently separating them. 'Come on, let's just sit down quietly and not get sacked....' He turned to the offended locals. 'Sorry lads, it's all good.'

Elsie turned round to where her sister was swaying. She quietly whispered to Faith. 'And you. What were you thinking?'

'I just wanted to join in,' Faith said quietly. 'I thought it would be funny.'

'Does it look like they are laughing? We're here to work. You've just caused a scene.'

Elsie looked at Blake and Zoe, who were quietly looking at each other. 'I'm sorry about this.' The awkward atmosphere hung between them all like a fog.

'Don't worry about it, mate,' Blake said. He gave her a slight smile before his gaze returned to his tankard.

Elsie bit her lip. 'Faith, go upstairs to our room.' Faith looked like she would protest for a moment before storming off upstairs. Her eyes looked tearful.

'Let me buy you another drink,' Calvin offered.

'No, thank you. I've gone right off drinking. I'm going to chill out upstairs before the festival starts.' Elsie looked at the empty cider and mentally cursed. That had been a lie. Elsie hadn't gone off drinking. If anything, she could murder another cider. Maybe she could grab another after she got paid tomorrow.

Blake cheerfully broke the ice by talking about his adventures in his hometown.

Getting up, Elsie gave Calvin a venomous look. The lovely spring day had been utterly ruined. First, she had been robbed, then Faith and Calvin had conspired to ruin the drinks. This would've been a wonderful opportunity for her sister and her to pretend that they lived an everyday life.

'I'm going to disappear upstairs,' Elsie stood up. 'I'm not really in the mood to drink anyway.'

Zoe leaned in and whispered in Blake's ear. He gave a shy smile. 'I think we might go upstairs too,' Blake said.

'You are all leaving me on my own? I just got a round in.' Calvin looked around. 'Zoe has barely touched hers.'

Blake leant over and necked Zoe's cider, belching appreciatively. 'Much appreciated, mate. I'll be down later, I'll buy you one before we leave.'

They left Calvin looking into his cider. A bitter air surrounded him.

When they were halfway to the pub door, Zoe moved towards Elsie. 'So he is a psycho then. One in every team, I guess.'

'He is an entitled prick,' Elsie muttered. 'Thanks for protecting Faith, Blake. I really appreciated it. She is a good kid, just an idiot sometimes.'

'Aren't we all, mate? No worries.' Blake paused to awkwardly disengage from Zoe, the pub entrance being too narrow for them to enter entwined. Elsie patiently waited to let them handle the logistics.

'Do you want a pint to take upstairs, Elsie?' Blake asked. 'I don't mind getting you one.'

'Thank you, but I think I'm just going to go up and play with my phone.' Elsie watched as Zoe oozed over Blake and left them to it. They seemed oblivious to the previous drama. She headed upstairs. Her eyes narrowed as she entered the shared bedroom with Faith. Curled up on the bed, she slurred, 'I don't feel well.'

'You absolute idiot. What were you thinking?' Elsie sat next to her. Out of habit, she checked her forehead. It seemed fine.

'I've had cider before. This feels different. I can't move my legs.' Faith's voice was growing more slurred.

Elsie looked her up and down. 'Show me.' Faith moved her limbs. They twitched like a zombie. 'Any nausea?'

'No, just very sleepy,' Faith murmured in a barely legible tone.

Elsie brushed her hair out of her eyes. 'You wait here, poppet.'

Elsie calmly left the room, then, as soon as she closed the door, her eyes flared. Swearing, she stormed down the stairs. Blake and Zoe were just coming up.

'That prick drugged my cider. Faith is paralytic, zombified.' Zoe's eyes opened wide.

Blake held up his hands. 'Let's not jump to conclusions. She is only little. Maybe she just can't handle cider. It's quite strong.'

'This isn't her first pint, Blake, much as it should have been. Besides, she is fourteen, not six.' Elsie pushed past them.

'Elsie, wait.' Zoe grabbed her shoulder. 'Listen, he's going to get what's coming to him, but let's be smart about this, right?' Elsie turned to listen to Zoe. 'We need a fourth person to do this shitty festival, or they just might call the whole thing off. I can't afford to lose the five hundred pounds, can you? Please, Elsie.'

'If you think—' Fury blazed in Elsie's eyes.

'—We are going to confront him. But we aren't going to do anything stupid. We'll let him know that we know. Then after the festival we show him exactly how we treat sleaze balls that drug women,' Zoe said. 'Do you understand?'

'Fine. I'll keep it quiet, but I'm talking to him now.' Elsie looked around at the rest of the pub's inhabitants. 'Wouldn't want to upset the Last of the Summer Wine again, would we?'

'I'll come too,' Blake said evenly.

The three of them walked outside to where Calvin was sitting alone at the picnic table. He was muttering into his pint. Elsie sat opposite him, her face stormy. Blake sat next to him. He gripped Calvin's shoulder with vice-like strength.

'Get off.' Calvin jerked but couldn't dislodge the big man. 'What the—'

'Don't make a scene, Calvin. The only reason that I'm not kicking the living shit out of you is that we've a job to do and we need the money. Do you understand?' Elsie's eyes were ice-cold. They locked onto him as she repeated. 'Do you... understand?'

Calvin slumped. 'I haven't done—'

Zoe tossed a small baggy of tablets onto the table. 'Well well, just look at what he had in his pockets.'

'They are medicine.' Calvin muttered.

'In an unmarked baggy? Sure, go on then, take one.' Elsie urged.

Calvin looked around. 'I've already had my medicine today.'

Elsie leaned forwards. 'Stop lying. We know what you've done. Just admit it.'

Calvin's face darkened. 'It's so easy for chads like you.' He thumbed at Blake. 'You just got off the coach and immediately got laid. Women don't give a shit about the little guys. I didn't choose to be this height. What do you expect me to do?'

He looked at them all, then shook his head. 'I found the answer to my problems just a week ago. I might not be big like Blake, but I'm smarter. I'm cleverer than he'll ever be.'

Blake snorted.

Then Calvin told them a story about true love.

Chapter Two

27th April, 2013, Truro, Cornwall

'Calvin, right?' Turning around, Calvin saw Emily. His eyes widened. 'Do you remember me? I was in your year at school.'

Pulling out his spliff, his face flushed. 'Emily.' He more than remembered her. He had loved her from the shadows but never had the courage to ask her out. 'What are you doing here?'

Looking down at her textbooks, she cocked an eyebrow. 'The same as you, I'll wager. College.'

'Oh yeah, I mean, yeah, that makes sense.' *Stupid.* Calvin shuffled nervously on the spot.

'That cigarette smells interesting. Mind if I have a toke?' Emily smiled, her hair blowing in the Cornish sea breeze.

Calvin handed it over without thinking. 'Sure, it's good stuff. My mate knows the supplier.'

'I'm pretty new here. I don't suppose you fancy introducing me to the Student Union, do you?'

His heart thudded in his chest. *This is it. This is my one chance.* 'Sure.' *I can't screw this up. It has to be perfect.* 'Let's meet up later, say at four?'

'That sounds perfect. Four it is then.' Emily winked at him.

Calvin ditched class. Emily was his priority. Texting his mate, he gave him a shopping list of drugs. Then, showering, Calvin wet shaved. After drying off, he put on his Ben Sherman polo shirt and his cleanest pair of jeans. Lynx Java deodorant and Hugo Boss aftershave added the finishing touch.

It was close to three. Calvin checked his phone and hurried out to meet his mate.

'You've quite the night planned.' His mate smirked.

Ignoring the snarky remark, Calvin asked, 'Have you got everything?'

'Ounce of weed, one Rohypnol, one Viagra. I have a gram of coke if you plan on going clubbing later. If you give me more time, I could get my hands on some MDMA.'

Calvin shook his head. *Perfect.* He handed over the money and shuffled over to the Student Union.

Inside, The Pixies were playing as they found a table. Calvin's eyes flashed with excitement as she settled down. She had never seemed more beautiful.

'Fancy a drink?' he asked nervously. He had gamed this out in his head a hundred times, but now it was happening for real.

'Thank you, I'll have a cider please,' Emily replied as he had anticipated. *Yes, yes.*

He ordered a pint of Stella Artois for himself and a cider for Emily. Looking down at the drinks, Calvin had a moment of indecision. She seemed so relaxed and friendly in his company. *Could I win her over with my personality?*

The moment ended. Calvin's mind snapped shut, fuelled by a bitter cynicism. *Chads get the girls, those over six feet, with muscles, money and power.* He dropped the Rohypnol into her cider. *This is the only way you'll ever get to sleep with a girl as flawless as Emily.* Love? That was reserved for other people, certainly not for the likes of him.

Regretfully, he handed the cider over to her. Ruefully, Calvin wished there was another way.

'Is everything alright?' Emily asked.

He smiled back at her. 'Yeah, it's all good.' Pointing at the cider, he said, 'It's Kopparberg, the good stuff.'

She drank the cider.

He only made it halfway through his pint before she began to stumble with her words.

'Let's grab some fresh air, eh?' Calvin suggested. 'A bit of a smokey smoke to chill out.'

'I'm really sorry. I guess I must have been more tired than I thought.' She nearly tripped. He caught her.

Leaning against the student union wall, they puffed on Calvin's spliff.

'I'm really sorry, Calvin, I'll make it up to you, but I think I need to get home,' Emily slurred.

'It's okay, I'll get a cab. Make sure you get home alright.' He had his arm around her, pulling her towards the taxi stand.

She texted him her home address, he swiped ignore on the notification screen. Lowering her into the taxi, he climbed in on the other side.

'If she is sick, it's a fifty quid fine,' the driver warned.

Calvin pulled out fifty in notes and showed the driver he had the cash. Emily reached for her wallet but fell unconscious. Calvin gave the driver his address. Then he popped the Viagra. *Thirty minutes to kick in*. The Viagra wasn't necessary. As he looked at his perfect angel, his body reacted immediately.

In the morning, he was lying in bed smoking a spliff. Emily's eyes widened as she woke in horror.

'I'm sorry, I didn't mean the night to end like this,' she mumbled, shaking her head. 'I just wanted a friend at college. This isn't what I'm like.'

'It's okay, I understand,' Calvin said honestly. *You'll end up with a doctor, a lawyer or a rugby player. Some men get all the luck, but at least I had one perfect night.*

She lumbered out of bed, nervously concealing her nakedness as she looked for her clothes.

He watched her, drinking in his last moments before the dream expired.

'I've got to go, but I will text you,' she promised, hurriedly finding the exit to his flat.

No, you won't. Calvin took a final puff before stamping out the roll-up.

He might not have won the genetic lottery, but he was self-aware. He knew how the world worked. Calvin just had to be more intelligent, more cunning than the chads of this world. Emily was a classic Stacy, a girl who would normally be forever out of his reach. Sighing, Calvin smiled. Some chad was going to be a very lucky man.

Not last night, though. He had beaten the system at its own game. The underdog isn't necessarily a bad place to be. Nobody ever suspects the quiet loser.

The letterbox banged. Getting out of bed, Calvin wandered towards the door. He picked up a cardboard invitation. He had been asked to read a script at a shitty country fair.

A guaranteed five hundred quid?

He chuckled. The universe was finally turning his way. This was proving to be the best week of his life.

Chapter Three

1st May, 2013, Huddersford, Kent

'**Y**ou are sick.' Elsie looked at Calvin. She felt ill seeing the worm's face. She rose and backed away from the table. 'I'm going upstairs to look after Faith. I can't wait for this whole horror story of a festival to end.'

Blake let go of Calvin, who glared at him. A mixture of shame and indignation was painted across Calvin's face as he sniffed.

'Come on, Zoe, let's get another cider. We've a few hours until the festival starts. Let's make the most of it.'

Zoe, for once bereft of her customary salacious expression, solemnly rose. She looked at Calvin with disgust before grabbing her bag to join Elsie and Blake as they headed back to the pub.

Elsie was watching from the pub entrance. Calvin had been unmasked, another predator in a world of them. He might have escaped justice this time, but she was on to him, as were the others. She and Faith had been through enough. This was just yet another piece of evidence that nobody could be trusted. They could only rely on each other. The sooner they did the job, the sooner they could leave.

She looked around. The sun shone brightly on the happily drinking residents and she wondered what other rot hid in this village. *Or did we just bring it with us?* It wasn't a happy thought.

Leaving Zoe and Blake at the bar, she returned upstairs to where Faith was sleeping. Curling up behind her, she stroked her hair until it fell away from her face.

Elsie didn't know how long she lay there until she fell into a dreamless nap, but her phone eventually woke her up, chirping softly beside her. Faith continued to sleep, gently snuffling on the pillow beside her. Elsie looked at her, concerned. She reached over to wipe off a patch of drool from her mouth. After assuring herself that she would be ok, she placed the spare key on the bedside table next to her, then went to the bathroom at the end of the corridor to clean her face.

It was showtime.

Picking up the laminated sheet from Geoff, she looked at the instructions.

Dresscode: Rough, warm clothes for outdoor activity. Sensible shoes or boots. After the performance, there will be a ceremonial chase through the woods, so don't wear restrictive garments.

She pulled a face as she got to the end of the page.

We take this festival very seriously, but that doesn't mean it isn't tremendous fun. So go out there and have a great time.

Her experience with Calvin had utterly killed the atmosphere of fun for her. She would keep an eye on him, then she'd run straight back to the pub and Faith and she would get the first coach out of here.

Where do we go next?

Elsie dismissed the thought. Pulling tight her hoodie, she looked in the mirror. Elsie had no makeup with her, no perfume. Washing her face, she did the best she could to get presentable. If Elsie hadn't needed the money so badly, she would have unleashed hell on Calvin. As it was, she would just have to be careful.

Taking a deep breath, she braced herself for the quaint country rituals in which she was about to partake. TV had warned her that it was likely to be both utterly inane and totally dull.

Leaving the room and locking the door behind her, Elsie knocked on Zoe's door. It creaked open. *She must be with Blake, or otherwise downst–*

The picture frame.

Barging the door open, she marched in and saw her picture frame poking out of Zoe's bag. Picking up the bag and upending it, she saw iPods, mobile phones, wallets and all kinds of knick-knacks.

'What are you doing in my room?' A panicked voice came from behind her. She turned to look at the nervous face of Zoe, with Blake as a shadowy figure before her.

'I *was* looking for you, but what I actually found was my picture. What the fuck, Zoe?' Elsie pointed at the contents of the bag.

Blake stepped forwards. 'Zoe, what did you do?' His face fell. He turned to Zoe, looking hurt.

Zoe moved towards the bed and shovelled everything into her bag. 'I didn't know any of you when I took them.'

'That is no defence. I don't know you but I haven't stolen your stuff?' Elsie raged. 'You stood there with us while we judged Calvin and all the time you've been picking our pockets.'

'It is not the same! He is a rapist. I just do what I do to survive.' Zoe sat down on the bed, her face in her hands. 'You have it easy.' She sobbed.

'Easy? You have no idea what Faith and I have been through. Easy?' Elsie's eyes narrowed. *Calvin, now Zoe. What are you hiding, Blake? When are you going to betray us?*

'Talk to us, Zoe. What is going on?' Blake said with a tenderness and warmth that annoyed Elsie even more.

Chapter Four

29th April, 2013, Elephant and Castle, London

'Zoe, Zoe! Come over and meet Roger.' Her mother, Danielle, waved her over, slopping Pinot Grigio onto the already stained carpet.

Zoe had just returned from school. Dumping her bag, she ignored the drunken couple. She didn't need to meet Roger. Roger was a place-holder, a cardboard template that was replaced nightly by whatever man had bankrolled his mother's drinking down the pub.

She went straight to the kitchen. Opening the fridge, she saw a generic bottle of vodka in the freezer and two bottles of Sainsbury's Pinot Grigio chilling in the fridge compartment. Nothing edible at all. Not even any milk to make a bowl of cereal for dinner.

'Have a drink with us, Zoe!'

Zoe returned to the living room. Looking straight at Roger, she asked him directly, 'Do you have any money? We have no food in the kitchen. I'm going to the shops.'

Her mother squawked, slamming her abused wine glass onto the pine side table. She tried to stand up and failed. 'What a thing to say! Roger dear, I'm so sorry . You know how kids get.' Slumping back on the sofa, she resigned herself to staring with indignation. 'Why don't you just go out and play, like a normal kid.'

'I'm seventeen, Mum. You are supposed to tell me to do my homework. To prepare for my A-levels. To go to bed early.' Zoe ignored her mother's protest and walked straight out of the house. She needed food, but more than that, she needed to get away from the decaying corpse of an uncaring addict.

One of the benefits of being seventeen was free travel. Zoe headed to Lambeth. Her headphones on, she settled back on a tube. A suited man leered at her. She ignored him. Unlike her mother, she already knew which men had something to offer and which were just looking for someone to take advantage of.

Emerging from the tube station at Lambeth, Zoe started to head towards a corner shop she knew from experience had poor CCTV. She had built up in her head a list of such shops that she could reliably use when the money ran out.

A young lad offered her a cigarette. She smiled at him, accepting the gift. 'My name is Jacob,' he said, his voice stuttering as he failed to maintain eye contact with her. His hand flicked back the curly tussles of his hair.

She stroked his arm gently.

An easy mark.

'You can see everyone heading to the O2 Academy in Brixton from this bench. It's like a window into another world.'

Zoe nodded, smiling at him. 'You are so deep, Jacob. You speak like a poet .'

'I er, thank you. I like to read but have written nothing so far.' He looked down at his feet, smiling awkwardly. One foot started tapping a rhythm on the path.

Her hand brushed at an imaginary piece of lint on his hoodie. 'I like you, Jacob. You are so smart. Why don't we go to the Maccas over the road? Get a burger and get to know each other.'

His eyes lit up. For the first time, he could hold Zoe's gaze, if only for a moment. 'I'd love to, but I don't have any money. I have a Twix, though.' He held out the bar.

'Jacob, that is so kind.' *Worthless.* She took the Twix, favouring him with a smile, and stood up. 'I have to get some stuff for home. It was nice meeting you.'

Jacob's face fell. She walked past him without looking back. Zoe felt as indifferent to Jacob as she did to the homeless people who asked her for change. They were just more people who wanted something from her. Why should she offer herself to someone who had nothing to offer in exchange? She opened up the Twix and took a bite.

She reached her chosen quarry, the Quality Superstore. A cramped cupboard of a shop. The greedy owner had stacked the shelves in the centre too high, so they blocked the CCTV camera. The door opened with its habitual ding, then her face fell. They had installed a second camera.

Bastards.

Zoe backed out. Mentally, she reviewed her options. There was a 'cash and carry' in Pimlico, a short bus ride away. She looked for the closest stop. It was right next to... she had forgotten his name already but knew it would be awkward, so walked up the road in the other direction to find the next stop on the route.

A drunken old man had fallen asleep at the bus stop. She could see his wallet poking out from his pocket. Sliding down next to him, she slipped the wallet into her jacket as he woke, peering at her with bleary eyes.

'Hello mate, are you ok? You fell asleep. Do you have some water on you?' Zoe smiled at him as he looked around, disorientated. He jabbered something in an Australian accent, then reached into his bag to pull out a battered plastic bottle with some water. 'What bus are you looking for?'

He blathered something incoherent and she nodded at him. 'I'll check that on my phone for you.'

When he looked away, she walked off quickly round the corner. Pulling out the wallet, she threw away the cards and pocketed the cash. Forty quid. Not a bad score. She tossed the empty wallet and walked towards Vauxhall to grab some food for dinner and head home.

It was dark when she arrived back at the house. She nearly missed it, but something caught her eye. She did a double-take when she saw the cardboard invitation lying on the doormat.

'When did this—' Of course, her mother was asleep on the sofa. Roger had left her top pulled down, exposing a breast. He was long gone.

She walked into the kitchen to run a glass of water and looked at the invitation. Five hundred pounds just to read out some lines at a weekend play.

Five hundred pounds... not enough to get a flat, but food wouldn't be a problem for a while.

Chapter Five

1st May, 2013, Huddersford, Kent

E lsie listened to the tale, her face deadpan. She regarded Zoe with a stone-cold expression. She shook her head. 'We've all had a bad time. Faith and I had to run away from home. You left by choice. We get by hand to mouth, sometimes we sleep in the street, but we don't steal. There is never any excuse for breaking the law.'

'Oh great, listen to you, Mrs Pure As Driven Snow. If I'd stayed at that house for a moment longer, I'd have gone insane. Can you blame me for seizing an opportunity when it presented itself?' Zoe still had tears running down her face. Blake sat down and awkwardly put his arm around her.

Elsie blinked. 'What? Still? Just because she didn't steal from you. She is still using you.'

'You don't know that, Elsie. Life isn't black and white. I've done bad things in my life as well.' Blake hugged Zoe tight.

'Sometimes, we do bad things for the right reasons. Have you never broken the law? Not once?'

Elsie avoided the question. 'Alright, Zoe, I'm taking *my* photo back to my room where it will stay. Then I'll meet you both in the corridor. Clean yourself up. We have a job to do. Then Faith and I are getting as far away from this bloody village as possible.'

Elsie opened the door and put the family photo on the bedside table next to the sleeping form of Faith. She looked at the girl, so innocent, yet Elsie had brought her into this nest of vipers.

Backing out gently, she locked the door and tested it to ensure she was secure. A few moments later, Zoe and Blake emerged. Zoe didn't make eye contact with Elsie as they headed downstairs. Elsie forced herself to remain calm when she saw Calvin at the bar making small talk with Geoff.

The little things in life do not bother me.

It was something her mum used to say. Whenever things seemed dark, she would set her shoulders and say it. She had a way of separating the world's harsh realities from her life. *A defence mechanism.* These days, Elsie felt she couldn't do that. Life was crashing against her soul like the coastal tide, eroding her. Each day she felt less.

Now, she was pretending to be a hare to amuse some villagers alongside a rapist and a thief. *What did Blake mean when he said they'd all broken the law? What was his sin?* She set her shoulders, raised her chin, and approached Geoff and Calvin.

The little things in life do not bother me.

'Elsie, my hare! How are you feeling? Rested, full of excitement for the stage?' Geoff beamed at her.

Oh, fuck off, you prissy prick.

'I can't wait. I've rehearsed my lines.' Elsie plastered a fake smile on her face.

'Wonderful, wonderful, wonderful. I see the makings of a true professional actor in you.' As Zoe and Blake came up behind Elsie, he spread his arms wide. 'We are all here. This is magnificent news. I am so very excited about tonight. A bi-centennial faire, secret mysteries, music, dancing, action. Come, come, come!' Geoff swooped towards the pub exit. Calvin sculled his cider. He was swaying as he followed Geoff.

Great, the idiot is drunk already. He had better not mess this up any more than he already has. Elsie followed them out to where Geoff was standing by a battered Land Rover.

The pub was getting busier as people tanked up in preparation for the festival.

Geoff drove them down the road. A pair of villagers opened a gate for him as the Land Rover meandered down a long field sidetrack. Sitting in the back of the vehicle on metal benches, they bounced along uncomfortably.

'I don't think this is legal,' Blake muttered as they bounced over a pothole. 'We don't have any seat belts. No, this absolutely can't be legal.'

Elsie shrugged. 'Five hundred pounds. I'll take a few bumps for that. Faith and I can survive for two, maybe three weeks on that.'

'Two weeks after rent? That is a bit bleak, isn't it? What do you eat? Noodles?' Blake looked sympathetically at her.

'Ramen noodles, beans on toast, cereal, cheese on toast, and baked potatoes. Actually, you'd be surprised at how easy it is to live on very little.' Elsie smiled ruely.

Zoe sniffed. 'I'm not sure that is actually living. Sounds like school dinners to me.'

'We don't all have access to your *alternative* sources of income.' Elsie looked accusingly at Zoe. 'We take what we can get.'

'I suppose,' Blake said, 'I am lucky, in a way.'

'How so?' Elsie asked.

Blake looked off for a while, gazing at someone or something that didn't exist.

'Well, it sounds bad, but it isn't, really.'

He began:

Chapter Six

18th March, 2013, near Kingston, Jamaica

The deck gently swayed underneath them as he watched Mr James Dyke croon through Suspicious Minds. Beside him, his gran was entranced by the performance. He smiled. Elvis wasn't his thing. Blake was more of an Ed Sheeran fan, but the cruise had been a magical experience. A year ago, his gran had found cheap tickets for a cruise around the Caribbean and it was proving to be the holiday of a lifetime. He gratefully accepted another complimentary lager from the waiter. Unlimited buffet food, unlimited drinks. Blake was definitely getting his money's worth. His gran always said his stomach was a bottomless pit and he happily proved her correct.

The Elvis impersonator finished his set to the applause of the crowd. Blake put down his chicken wing bone and clapped happily. Then, looking at the state of his hands, he looked around for a napkin. Without taking her eyes off the stage, his gran handed him a pack of tissues from her bag.

'I wish I'd seen him live,' she confessed. Sipping at her wine, she reached into her bag for a couple of aspirin. The DJ started playing. He listened to the track, trying to place it. His gran saw his look of confusion and patted his arm. 'Nat King Cole, dear. 'When I fall in love'.'

He grinned at her. 'Thanks, I thought I recognised it from your albums.' He plied the bowl for a final cheesy chip and after some ferreting, he found part of a chip at the bottom. He chucked it into his mouth and crunched down on it.

For the hundredth time, he said to her, 'This was a genius idea, gran.'

She beamed at him, then slowly stood up. He reached out to help her up. 'You stay and enjoy the music. I'll see you at breakfast.' Blake gave her a gentle hug. She reached up to tussle his hair.

'Gerroff, you'll mess up the gel!' He pulled back as her eyes sparkled.

As she tottered back to her room, Blake supped his lager and looked around the room. He spied a pair of girls he had drunk with the night before. He raised his glass as they waved to him. He rose with a grin and headed over to catch up with them.

He woke to his alarm clock. Showering, he quickly dressed and headed down to the restaurant. His gran was nowhere to be seen. An early riser, he would always find her at a window seat with a pot of tea.

Always.

Concerned, he returned to her cabin and knocked. When there was no response, he dialled her mobile and prayed she had remembered to charge it. Blake felt sick when he heard the phone ring unanswered in her room. Racing for a cabin crew member, he persuaded them to open the door.

He wished he hadn't.

Blake lay alone in his cabin. His gran's body had been transferred off the ship when they docked at Jamaica.

What was he to do?

His gran wasn't just his only known relative, she was his best friend. Now he was all alone. His phone trilled repeatedly. The texts from the girls onboard went unanswered as he slipped into a dark depression.

Chapter Seven

25th March, 2013, Stratford, London

The plane flight back to London had been uneventful. A small child had kicked the back of his seat and his headphones hadn't worked, but none of that mattered. What did matter was returning to their flat to find it full of memories. He grabbed a coke from the fridge and sat in his favourite armchair. Turning on Netflix, he put it on shuffle.

When he felt hungry, he went to the fridge. It was empty. Picking up his phone, he ordered a pizza and returned to his armchair, sipping on a can of coke. Looking around for a napkin, he turned by reflex to his gran's chair. It was vacant. He sighed and got up to wash his hands in the kitchen.

It was nearly a month later when he needed to get cash. Pulling on his hoodie, he trundled into town to find an ATM. He mutely pressed for a statement after removing a hundred pounds from the machine. Blake blinked and peered again at the scrap of paper. His gran's full pension had been deposited yesterday. A big smile crossed his face. Despite the crisp air, warmth flowed through him. Even from beyond the grave, she was still looking after him.

He hadn't been abandoned.

With the money he'd taken from the ATM, he went to a nearby café and ordered a full English breakfast and a large pot of tea. He filled two cups and put the second opposite him. Clinking it with his mug, he smiled. 'Thanks, Gran. I miss you so much. I hope you've taught them how to make a good cuppa in heaven.' He chuckled. 'I bet you've seen Elvis perform live now.'

The next day, his luck continued to grow. An invitation to perform at the Festival of Masks appeared on his doorstep.

Chapter Eight

1st May, 2013, Huddersford, Kent

'So, wait. The day after you spent your gran's pension money, the invitation arrived?' Elsie asked. 'And the same thing happened to you two?' Elsie looked at Zoe and Calvin. They looked at each other and nodded. 'I'm getting a bad feeling about this. How did they find us anyway? I thought they had just randomly sent out invitations.'

'They must have.' Zoe squinted. 'I mean, nobody knows what we did. Right.'

Elsie looked thoughtful. 'I suppose.'

Calvin looked suspiciously at Elsie. 'Following your logic. That means you know you did something.'

'I didn't say that,' Elsie said sharply.

'I mean, if these invitations came after we'd committed a crime.' Calvin frowned. 'That means you must have committed one if you got an invitation.'

'Well, I didn't commit a crime.' Blake grinned amiably.

They all looked at him. 'You are a benefits cheat. That is fraud,' Calvin muttered.

'No. It's my gran's money. She would have wanted me to have it. We took care of each other.' Blake looked hurt. 'I'd never break the law. I am a good man.'

Zoe moved to sidle into his chest, but he shrugged her off. She moved away with a wounded expression.

'Seriously. I have never broken the law in my life.' Blake was looking cross now. 'Don't put me in the same bracket as the other two.'

'Hey!' Zoe punched him in the shoulder. 'What the fuck was that about?'

'So now you are better than us, are you?' Calvin sneered. 'You are a cheat, mate, a fucking fraud.'

Elsie looked at Calvin. 'Everyone is better than you. You rapist twat.'

The Land Rover stopped as Calvin's face darkened. They ceased their arguing as they looked around with trepidation.

They had reached their destination.

They were in an old forest clearing. It was filled with a heaving mass of people laughing and drinking. Some of them Elsie recognised from the pub.

Unlike the rest of the orchard, the trees here weren't fruit.

They were encircled by yew trees. Far older and more prominent than the rest, a giant yew loomed over an ancient stone table. It was engraved with a strange runic pattern of grooves on its top. Overlooking the centre of the clearing was a large wooden stage with lighting set up on steel scaffolding. A whole hog was being roasted over coals, on a spit to the left of them. A bar had been set up with huge cider barrels to their right. The spiced scent of cooked pork with cloves and the sweet smell of fermented apples hung in the air. A DJ was playing the Rolling Stones.

Geoff opened the Land Rover doors, his face glowing with excitement.

'Come, come, my beauties, we have a tented area set up behind the stage where you can prepare yourselves. In two hours when the time is nigh, I'll need you to put on your masks and assemble on the stage. The order of assembly is from left to right, stage left, that is, it's marked on your sheets.'

'What's stage left?' Blake asked.

'As you stand basking in the audience's adulation,t it is to the left of you.' Geoff pointed at the stage.

'I'll show you where to stand.' Zoe stroked his shoulder.

Blake refused to look at her. 'No thanks, I'll figure it out for myself.'

Elsie tapped Geoff on the side. He spun theatrically and beamed beneficently at her. 'Geoff, why were *we* chosen specifically? How did you get our addresses? What would have happened if one of us had said no?'

'Good golly, what excellent questions. A fine mind you have, my young hare. Sharp as a razor.' He looked around the milling crowd. 'There! Jack, he is your man,' Geoff whispered conspiratorially. His whisper was still deafeningly loud. 'He is the Avatar of Cernunnos.' Geoff pointed to a serious-looking bespectacled man in a suit. The Avatar waved politely at them. 'He is an accountant by trade. The orchard chose him. It's an old tradition. The trees are supposed to whisper the actors' names and how to find them.'

Elsie traded glances with Blake. Both seemed unconvinced.

Ignorant of their concerns, Geoff erupted into a sudden and sharp bout of laughter. He slapped the sides of his ample belly. 'Hogwash, I'm sure. I think he just gets his secretary to handle the role of recruitment, between you and me. Maybe she uses Google or TikTok or something... 'internetty''.' He wiggled his fingers to indicate someone using the arcane rituals of accessing the internet. 'We probably had a few pull-outs before we found you but best to play along. They take their rituals very seriously here.'

'And the chase?' Elsie asked.

'The best bit! When Jack blows on his horn, it's an antique, you know, you must all scamper between those two trees marked by ribbons. Once through them, you can follow any route you choose just so long as you arrive back at the pub within three hours. If you do, there will be the two hundred and fifty-pound bonus and you'll be able to remove the mask.'

'Do we get a head start?' asked Blake.

'Of course! You get a five minute head start.' Geoff leaned in. 'It is only fair, as the locals know the terrain very well and are a touch more athletic than you soft city types.' He laughed, rubbing his belly. 'Believe it or not, I used to be an athletic whippersnapper myself. I was too young to be at the last festival, though. It seems draconian, but you have to be eighteen to be a hound. Still, the times they are a-changin. You know this is the first year we've allowed women!'

'How progressive of you,' Zoe said, her voice devoid of any emotion. 'You must be so proud.'

Calvin was scanning the forest. 'They won't be rough, will they?'

'How on earth do you mean, my wee boy?' Geoff rubbed his shoulder enthusiastically. 'It's touch rules. If you get even the slightest touch by a hound, you are out of the game.'

Leaving them to go backstage, he headed back to the Land Rover. Calling over his shoulder, he warned, 'Remember, the Wild Hunt will chase you. If any of them touch you, you are no longer eligible for the bonus, but you get to remove your mask and join the party. This is all on the briefing sheet.'

Elsie watched Geoff get into his vehicle and drive away. 'Come on then.' She headed towards the backstage tent, Zoe in tow. Looking behind her, she could see the boys lingering. 'Come on, let's get this shit show over with.'

'Well, you see.' Blake said hesitantly.

Calvin pointed at the cider stand. 'It is free.'

Shaking her head, Elsie left them. Calvin was already drunk, but there was little she could do about it. Elsie just hoped he didn't mess it up for the rest of them. She needed that money.

Walking into the tent, she found four tables, each one with a large wooden mask. Elsie beelined to the table with her white hare mask. It was lacquered and decorated with runes and iron studs. She turned it over in her hands. It was an ugly thing. A pair of leather straps dangled from the back. A padlock was next to it. She picked it up dubiously.

'I'm not wearing this.' Zoe shook her head. 'It's horrible. If they think they can padlock this thing to my face, they have another thing coming.'

'Yours looks better than mine. Mine looks sinister.' Elsie turned round the mask with its long wooden ears. 'They'll see me a mile off. Look at these massive white things.'

The boys entered and saw the masks. 'Cool,' Blake said. Both he and Calvin marched up to the badger mask. 'What do you think you are doing? You agreed to wear the pheasant mask.'

'They'll think I'm gay. Look at it. It's multi-coloured with glitter.' Calvin reached for the badger mask only to find his wrist held in a vice-like grip. 'Oh, come on.'

Zoe sauntered over to look. 'What's wrong with being gay, anyway?'

'Well, you aren't. You'll shag any bloke with a pulse,' Calvin muttered.

Blake turned around and lifted him by the throat.

'Put him down!' Zoe pulled at his arm. 'What is wrong with you?' After a moment's pause when he stared deep into Calvin's eyes, Blake dropped him. Calvin gasped, reaching out to the table for support. 'What? You ignore me for the entire drive here and then think you can protect me? What the fuck is wrong with you?'

'We are almost done here. Then we never have to see each other again.' Elsie gently pushed the boys apart. She subconsciously wiped the hand that touched Calvin on her hoody. His eyes followed her as she returned to her dressing room table.

'Could we attach them but just not use the padlocks?' Elsie wondered.

Zoe smiled. 'I have safety pins.'

'They won't be strong enough. You need string.' Blake was turning the mask over and analysing the buckles.

Elsie looked up. 'Do you think they'll let us?'

'I think it's worth a try. How close do you think the organisers will be checking,' Blake said, smiling. He shrugged. 'Let's give it a go, eh?'

'Let's not, eh?' From the tent entrance came a stocky blonde lady. 'I'm Jess, your hair and makeup girl.' She paused to pose. Elsie looked at her dubiously.

'I have my own makeup,' Zoe said, her face horrified.

'Jolly good, well, I won't do it against your will, but I will check to ensure that you are presentable before you go out.' She walked around them, taking each of the masks and putting them back in their places. 'Lovely. They look a lot older than they really are. They were made fifty years ago for the last festival. Except for the hare one, that's new for this year. It's a replica of the original. I helped make it. '

'They are very heavy.' Zoe picked hers up. 'Plastic would be lighter.'

'We carved them out of wood from our very own orchard. It's all part of the tradition.' Jess stroked the hare mask. 'You are very honoured to take part. It's all the community can talk about. You are as close to royalty as it gets around here.'

Flicking her hair, Zoe put on a posh voice. 'Well, I always suspected I would make a rather good princess.'

Elsie snorted.

'Do we have to memorise these lines?' Calvin was looking at his laminated briefing card. 'It's a lot of words.'

'It's one paragraph, Calvin. You can manage that surely?' Elsie had picked hers up and was mumbling her lines under her breath.

'Who wrote these?' Calvin laughed, looking at the archaic language. 'The BBC? This some kind of Shakespeare shit.'

Nobody answered him. The room was silent as Jess stared at him. Eventually, Jess said in an even mannered tone. 'These are sacred words. They are traditional and mean a great deal to our village. This is a serious role. If you don't treat it with the dignity that it deserves, then you'll be down the road.'

'Why didn't you hire proper actors?' Elsie asked.

'We did.' Jess gestured at the four of them.

Elsie rolled her eyes. 'By proper actors, I meant trained actors. For the money you are offering, you should have been able to get some that are at least formally trained, even if they lack experience.'

'You act every day. You are acting now.' Jess smiled. 'Every-one acts. You were chosen.'

Zoe approached her. 'How were we selected? I didn't sign up with any agencies. How did you find us?'

Shrugging, Jess waved her hands in dismissal. 'That isn't my department, dear. I'm hair and makeup. Now, will you be needing any of that, or do you want privacy to practise your lines?'

Blake was looking at his card. 'I could use some time to get my head around these lines.'

'...and of course, we'll need your phones.' Jess held out a small wicker basket.

Zoe recoiled. 'I think not.'

'Do you think Dame Judi Dench carries her phone onto the stage with her? Just in case she needs to reply to one of Kenneth Branagh's tweets?' Jess waved the basket again.

'There is no signal here anyway.' Elsie pulled out her phone. It was battered with a cracked screen. 'How do we get them back?'

'Geoff will have them at the pub. You'll get them with your cheque.' Jess took the phone and dropped it in. Grudgingly, the others added their own phones.

Jess turned and as she left the tent, she called over her shoulder. 'I'll be back in thirty minutes to help you with your masks.'

'I don't like this.' Zoe sat down at her dressing table and poked her mask. 'It doesn't make sense. We've been chosen? For what? Has any of us done any drama since secondary school?'

'You said it earlier. We are all criminals,' Calvin muttered.

'I'm not,' Blake protested.

'Whatever, Blake. Look, we should cut and run. This is weird. I don't like it.' Calvin was cut off by Elsie.

'We are doing this. Let's just stand outside, say our lines and then let them chase us for a few minutes to give them some fun. Then we take our five hundred pounds and get out of here.'

'Seven hundred and fifty. The hounds will never catch me. I'm going to beeline for the pub. I'll be there within half an hour. I'm a good runner,' Blake boasted, his voice matter of fact.

Zoe batted her eyelids at him and pouted. 'You wouldn't leave me behind, would you?'

'Well, you robbed everyone. So yeah. I wish you well and all, but you are on your own, mate.' Blake refused to meet her eyes.

Zoe bit her lip and stormed off to her desk.

'Come on then, let's get together and go through these lines until we can do them from memory without mistakes.' Elsie took up her position in the centre of the room.

'No, it's obvious that I'm not wanted.' Zoe started to cry softly. Guilt crossed Blake's face. He took a step towards her, but then went to join Elsie.

'Yeah, screw you guys.' Calvin went to his mirror and started to rehearse his lines independently.

Elsie and Blake had got it down to a stilted yet formal level. They could recite the words without the cards, though Elsie, while not being an expert, still felt it lacked depth or any form of emotion. None of them wanted to be there and it showed.

Jess arrived and watched misty-eyed as Elsie, then Blake, finished their lines. 'Oh, they chose well.'

'What is this 'audience reacts' at the end?' Zoe pointed at her briefing card.

Jess smiled as she picked up Zoe's mask. 'Oh, the audience will then say, 'We forgive you your sins.'

'Our sins?' Zoe said, her voice tinged with uncertainty.

'It's a purification ritual. We forgive the animals that do harm to our orchard and then ritually chase them with our 'hounds.' Just a bit of fun. Now, let's get the masks fixed on.' Zoe backed away. 'Just a couple of minutes on the stage, a romp in the woods and you get paid. Dead easy.'

Zoe fidgeted but allowed Jess to attach the mask. The padlock clicked shut with an echoing sound. It reminded Elsie of a gunshot.

Elsie watched as Blake had his badger mask fixed. Calvin complained that it was too tight, but was duly ignored by Jess. Then it was Elsie's turn. She looked at the wooden mask with distaste as it was picked up and strapped to her head.

Her world became two small eyeholes. Her breathing echoed loudly behind the wooden mask. It weighed down heavily, straining her neck. The musty, chemical scent of treated wood enveloped her. She fought down panic. Her peripheral vision was limited as she looked around.

I don't like this, I don't like it at all.

'Well, don't you all look lovely,' Jess said as she manoeuvred them towards the exit.

The cool evening air was refreshing on Elsie's face. It needed to be. The crowd that she could barely see through the eye holes cheered her on. All the attention caused her stomach to lurch. Whoops, clapping and cheers washed over her in a cavalcade of sound. The scent of food and spilt alcohol filled the air.

She was guided up the short stairs onto the stage, where the Avatar of Cernunnos stood in a black suit and white shirt, peering out at her through a huge stag's head.

What the hell?

The stage lights were overly bright. Elsie blinked to compensate. She automatically moved to her position as the other animals shuffled into place around her.

The Avatar raised his hands and the crowd fell silent.

'This year is a year of great celebrations. We have kept up our tradition, built up over the last twenty-three years, of winning the Gold Medal for Cider from the Campaign for Real Cider. Also, as we have over the last eight years, once again we have picked up the Gold Medal from the British Cider Association and for the very first time during our long established history of cider-making, we have been awarded the Good Housekeeping Best British Drink award. The Apple and Pear will have to add more shelves for our new intake of awards. In these troubled times, I urge you all to remember that this festival exists to protect us all from the perils of poverty that plague this land. Cernunnos is our guardian. We owe everything to him.' The audience applauded on cue. The Avatar waited for a respectful silence in which to offer his booming proclamation, then announced:

'From the distant times of yore, when our forefathers reigned, our lands were plagued by the four pests. The Fox, the Badger, the Hare and the Pheasant. In lean times, they created the Festival of Masks to renew our ancient link to the gods of old--'

'Heathen!' came from the audience. Elsie traced it to the vicar who was laughing into his cider cup. The crowd joined him in laughter.

'--who rewarded our faith with fertile harvests of the best fruits in Britain.' Rousing applause rose from the audience until he signalled them to be quiet. The DJ started to play a gentle orchestral soundtrack. The sounds of a fiddle could be heard playing a haunting tune.

Zoe stepped forward first with a flourish. 'I the Fox, hunt your livestock. No fence nor wall can keep me out.' Clawing her hands in the air, she gave a raw sound, much to the crowd's amusement.

The audience joined together to chant, 'We absolve you of your sins.'

Blake stepped forward and in perfect monotony, he bowed before booming. 'I the Badger, befoul the grounds with my tunnels and slaughter any dog sent to hunt me.'

Another chant of, 'We absolve you of your sins,' rose from the audience.

Elsie took up her position and chanted, 'I the Hare, feast on your crops and destroy your fields.'

'We absolve you of your sins,' the crowd shouted.

Calvin was last. 'I the pheasant, consume your grapes, eat your young shoots and bathe in dust, crushing your crops.'

The crowd was shouting louder now. 'We absolve you of your sins.'

The Avatar raised his hands to speak again. 'As before, so it is now. We have identified the four pests, the evils that plague our lands. It is time to expunge them.' Elsie saw large groups of people wearing terrifying hound masks at both sides of the stage. Unmistakably hounds, they were painted with nightmarish visages, huge fangs, bloody maws. In their hands were short staves. Each one ended with a runic bone cross.

'You will now open the path, so the prey may flee. Hold fast, my hounds. Without a challenge, the gods won't be honoured.'

Why do they need weapons?

Elsie shook as she looked down at the pack of hounds, dressed in hoodies and fleece jackets. They seemed to be champing at the bit, eager to get to grips with the young actors. The crowd opened up. A chorus of howls echoed from them, followed by the hounds, who were being held back by what looked like marshals.

'The prey will run, *now*.' The Avatar pointed. 'Run!' Blake was off, his long legs powering him through the crowd.

'Blake! Don't leave me,' Zoe wailed, as she ran after him, soon falling behind. Calvin jumped down from the stage and stumbled. He had misjudged the leap through alcohol or sheer accident. He must have twisted his ankle. Elsie could see him limping.

Elsie went for it. She ran through the whooping, howling crowd and tore through the woods in the direction of the pub.

They'll be expecting us to travel direct.

She veered off the path crashing through the foliage and bushes. Her ears kept being caught on the low lying branches.

They expect us to exhaust ourselves.

It's dark. Elsie had to outsmart them if she wanted the two hundred and fifty pounds. Blake might be out to outrun them, but she couldn't. Elsie found a large rhododendron bush. She shook her head to avoid getting those ears stuck and crept underneath it. She peered out through the thick foliage, catching a glimpse of the ongoing festivities, the dancing people and the cider-drinkers.

After a few minutes, she heard, 'Release the hounds!' The Avatar yelled to a chorus of howls. The hounds assembled in front of the festival-goers. Elsie blinked at the sudden brightness as they all turned on head torches. *You cheating bastards.* As they spread out into a fan, she watched them separate into three ranks. Then, group by group, they tore through the woods, one line sprinting, one line jogging and the other walking slowly, beating the bushes.

They take this far too seriously.

The first and second lines had torn past her, hurtling through the woods at breakneck speed. She saw one of the beaters heading towards her bush. Aware of just how white her mask was, she looked around, then lay down, placing her mask face down against the soil. She pulled the dead leaves and loam over the backs of her wooden ears and lay quite still. Motionless, she waited, not daring to breathe as the beater whacked the bush and peered inside.

Through luck, his incompetence or just the sheer size of the giant plant, he missed her and moved on. Elsie remained still for another minute, then raised her head to see what was happening. She was now behind the hunters. Grinning, she knew she had made it past the first trial.

Should have given me the Fox mask.

It didn't take long for the first howls of triumph to sound. She watched as a group of them came running back. She could see them carrying the limp form of— *You sick bastards.* The revellers back at the festival were stripping. The undulating forms of middle-aged farmers dancing around the altar were painfully visible. *They are sex people.* She shuddered as she watched the pale white flesh gleam in the firelight.

'And so we take the flesh of the Pheasant and as we sacrifice its heart to the woods, we forgive its sins.' Why was Calvin limp? Was he hurt? Then she heard the sickening sound of screaming. It was Calvin's voice. She knew then that he was dying. She had heard that sound before, at another time and another place.

She vomited. Most of it escaped through the breathing hole in her mask, but the rest dripped down her front. The smell of it filled her nostrils and she gagged. Her hands shook. The sick bastards were dancing naked as they killed Calvin. The music had changed to an orchestral track. It built up to a rhythmic pounding. The drums echoed through the woods like a powerful heartbeat. As they danced around his corpse, she shook her head in despair. As much as she hated him, he didn't deserve this.

This isn't justice.

She watched as several of the crowd, naked and drunk on cider and death, began rutting in the grass. Gorge threatened to rise again in her throat when a chill ran down her spine.

Faith is back at the pub alone.

Faith was unconscious, vulnerable. Who knows what they would do to her? She had to get back.

She had no doubt in her mind that what was waiting at the pub with cheerful Geoff was not a fat cheque. It was one of those bone truncheons.

Her jaw set. She waited until her breathing slowed. Then, with her body still shaking, she left the bush, staying low. She flitted from tree to tree. Ahead of her, she could see the lights of the hounds as they chased through the woods. She veered further to the left, always heading left, looking to outflank their lines and move around them. The hounds had fallen silent now. Their earlier howls had changed to quiet professionalism. Elsie pulled at the mask, but it was fixed on tight. Without a knife, she wasn't getting through those leather straps and even then, well, she risked cutting herself. For now, she quietly jogged through the night, her vision partially obscured, her nose filled with the scent of vomit, her ears reverberating with the sound of her own breathing.

If she had kept her phone, she could have tried to find some signal and dialled the police. As it was, it was down to her.

The wolf had been at the door before. Now it was back. Threats endangered her and, more importantly, Faith. Nothing would get in the way of saving her sister. The trees loomed like spectres in the dark. The moon was high and filtered through the leaves. An owl hooted. It was the least of the predators she had to worry about. She was overtaking the third line of hounds, the walkers. Curling around their left flank, she continued towards the pub.

She had emerged into the orchard. She could feel the squelch of rotten apples under her trainers and smell the sweet scent of dying fruit. The trees were more spread out and the undergrowth carefully hacked back, so that the cover was limited.

Creeping forwards, she saw the squat hives of the bees. Her ears strained to listen. It was all quiet except for the distant sounds of the chase over to her right. It was peaceful. Even the bees were sleeping.

Running forwards, she heard the howls of the hounds and watched as the lights concentrated on a point. Screams echoed into the night. Another of the prey had been caught.

Fuck. Fuck. Fuck.

She recognised Zoe's cries before they were abruptly cut off.

She looked around her. What would they do if they got to the pub and realised that she had eluded them? The pub must be guarded. This whole chase was rigged. Leaning against an apple tree, she caught her breath. If there was a ring of them around the pub, she was walking into a trap.

Is Faith already dead?

Maybe she should run for the coach station. The town was only another three miles away. She could make it before daybreak.

As she set off towards the pub, she hated herself for even considering leaving her sister. She had to rescue Faith or be sure that she was dead. She couldn't live with herself, knowing that she had abandoned her, not after everything they'd been through together.

As she jogged forward, she heard a rustling. Slowing, she listened again. It was quiet, other than her breathing echoing in the mask. She moved forward slowly. She heard it again to her left. She paused. Nothing. Starting off, she jogged, listening intently. A twig snapped. She turned and saw it. A hound with his head torch off. Of course, they'd have hidden hounds. She turned and ran immediately to the right. He howled as he pursued her and she watched as the lights in front of her turned towards her. They were still distant, but that wouldn't last long. She changed her trajectory to head towards the pub. As her trainers followed the dark path, the trees were a forest of dark silhouettes, a thousand obsidian fingers clawing at the sky.

A shadow flickered at her side and she turned too late. She was rugby tackled to the floor.

The hound raised his truncheon but then paused and got up. He managed two steps before Blake, in his badger mask, collided with him. Punching at the mask, Blake swore as it bruised and cut his knuckles. The hound screamed, his voice unexpectedly shrill in the quiet of the night. Rolling Blake off, he scrambled to his feet. He was looking for his truncheon when Elsie charged him, smashing him on the back of his head with his own weapon. With a sickening sound, bone crunched under the hardwood truncheon as she struck the hound repeatedly.

Blake's eyes widened as he heaved the dead weight of the hound off his own body . 'You... Is he dead?'

'This way,' she said, ignoring the question. Elsie led him further towards the pub. She could see it now, on the brow of the hill. Unfortunately, she could also see the hounds. It was like the whole world was chasing them. A forest of twinkling head torches.

'They got Zoe,' Blake muttered under his breath.

Elsie thought back to the stolen photo frame. It all seemed so petty now. 'They got Calvin too.'

'Some good has come of this then,' Blake said bitterly. To her surprise, Elsie didn't disagree.

'You know they'll be guarding the pub, don't you,' Elsie whispered, her voice ragged.

'I suspect so.' Blake jogged onwards. 'We don't have much choice, though.'

Elsie hated herself for what she was about to say. 'I have to make it to the pub. I need to get Faith, dead or alive. I need to know what's happened to her. You could run to the town, though, get the coach.'

'I've a better idea. I can draw the hounds off. You hide over by the fence. I'll start running back towards the woods. I can lose them in there and then tail back towards the town. You head to the pub. Get Faith, get out.' Blake's lips pressed together, he looked at the approaching head torches bitterly.

'That's... Why would you do that for me, Blake?' Elsie whispered.

Blake looked at her. 'I'm not a criminal. I'm not a bad man. These pricks, judging us, hunting us for entertainment, they are the real evil.' He rubbed his arms to ward off the cold. 'Now Zoe is dead. She asked me for help and I should have protected her. I... she didn't deserve that.' He bit his lip. 'It's time for me to start making the right decisions.'

Elsie didn't say anything. Instead, she hugged him. He turned to start running. 'Wait, Blake. I don't think you are a bad person. I think you have a good heart.'

Tears rolled down her face. He'd never know. The mask concealed everything.

He paused to listen, then started running. As he raced through the orchard, he must have become visible to one of the hounds as a chorus of howls echoed and Elsie saw the head torches turn his way. As the hounds ran past her position, she kept her mask facing down and waited for the silence to return. It must have been ten minutes before they had cleared her hiding spot. She hadn't heard any cries, so she could only hope Blake was still alive and safe.

She turned towards the pub and began circling it, the truncheon in her hand.

There were hounds placed around the pub still. Elsie could see them. She sat watching them patrol the building. When one of them paused, Elsie saw her opportunity and sprinted towards the gap in their perimeter. The hedge was hawthorn. She walked closer to the idle sentry until she found a small, albeit tight, hole. Gritting her teeth, she ignored the vicious thorns that slashed at her clothes and cut her skin. Her blood ran cold as she heard the hounds talking no more than a metre away.

'What the hell were you playing at?'

'I had to have a whizz, mate. That cider went right through me.'

She waited until her breathing had settled and they had moved on.

She was in the pub garden. Looking up, she could see the window of Faith's bedroom. She was close. The pub front door was open and light pooled out from inside.

Sliding around the side of the building, she tried the back door. Locked. The same with the kitchen.

Come on, I am so close!

The windows were all secured too. Looking at her truncheon, Elsie thought about smashing a window. But how do you do that quietly?

She made a decision. If you can't be stealthy then you have to be quick. She crept towards the open door and raced inside. Geoff was waiting. He was sitting in an armchair facing the door. A truncheon was in his hand.

A look of shock crossed his face. His mouth fell open at the sight of the truncheon she was holding.

'Now then, young lady, put that down and we'll see about getting you the prize you so richly deserve. Pretty little things like you shouldn't be running around with weapons.' He laughed, his eyes twinkling as he struggled to heave his ungainly body out of the depths of his comfortable armchair.

Elsie's eyes narrowed.

Chapter Nine

26th April, 2013, Clerkenwell Estate, London

E lsie lay waiting, dread and fear soaked deep into every fibre of her being. Her ears strained as she sought the sound that haunted her. The footsteps of her drunken father. Would he go left to pass out in his room? Or would he turn right to visit her room?

Taking deep breaths, she tried to calm herself by reciting her mantra. *Thirteen pounds, seventy-eight pence.* That was how much she had embezzled from the shopping budget. She could afford two one-way coach tickets for her and her younger sister Faith to escape to Portsmouth with sixteen pounds.

Elsie prayed that he wouldn't come tonight. The sweaty hands. The sharp alcoholic tang of his breath. The foul scent of tobacco clung to him. The bristly stubble that stung her skin.

Not tonight. Elsie would do anything for a night of peace.

She heard them.

The footsteps.

As her prayers reached a feverish crescendo, the worst thing that could possibly happen, happened.

Her prayers were answered.

Elsie's ears heard the screeching of the door handle, so quiet under normal circumstances, but tonight it felt deafening. It wasn't her door handle. It was her sister's.

What emotion was she expecting? Red hot rage? Cold icy terror? The anxiety that had filled her since her mother had left. The depression that had set in when the abuse began. It fled.

Elsie was left with a moment of crystal clear clarity. Her mind, razor-sharp, knew precisely what had to happen. Sliding out of bed, she opened her door quietly to see her father stalk into Faith's room.

Padding silently down the stairs, she crossed into the kitchen in pitch black. Feeling her way over to the knife rack, Elsie pulled out the large eight-inch cooks' knife before replacing it with the thinner, pointier, five-inch utility knife. Creeping up the stairs, she saw Faith's door open.

Knife outstretched, eyes forward, a steely determination to do what needed to be done filled her. As she entered, she found her father looming over Faith's bed, a mirror image of when he first came to her room, drunk. He was unsteady on his feet. Good, that would make this easier. Elsie paused, hatred for her abuser flowing through her veins as she heard Faith echo the words she had first uttered a year ago:

'Father? What are you doing?'

He was standing topless. *Good, no cloth to catch the blade.* Elsie clenched her grip tightly around the handle. Her mind clicked into place almost audibly as it committed to black murder. Stepping forward, she stabbed up under his ribs. He howled with surprise as the knife sunk deep into his side. He turned, eyes filled with anger.

Stab.

Stab.

Stab.

Ducking under his clumsy blow, Elsie stabbed the knife in again and again. She wasn't aiming for any location in particular. She just wanted him dead. Hot blood squirted. He gripped her tight as he collapsed. Foetid breath huffed into her face. His fingers clawed for her wrist.

In her memory, she was focused and analytical. Faith said otherwise. She remembered Elsie screaming and weeping with anger as she plunged the cold metal into his clammy flesh.

Elsie stopped only when the blade snapped off inside his body. It was only then that she realised the ogre was dead. Half rolling the corpse off, half wriggling out from under it, she looked at Faith. She was sitting up in bed, her eyes wide with terror.

'Faith, it's okay now. It's safe now.' Faith broke down in tears, shaking with fear and shock. Elsie was covered in blood, hot arterial blood drying to almost obsidian black in the dark. She took Faith gently by the hand. Leading her to the shower, the two sisters washed off the last remnants of the tyrant who had dominated their lives. Lying down in the shower well, they washed each other's hair. The warm, soapy water helped to loosen muscles taut with years of accumulated tension.

'We are free now, Faith,' Elsie promised. Faith was still crying. She had yet to say a single word, her thin, frail body rocking. As Elsie washed her hair, she seemed to calm.

'What will we do now?' Faith asked eventually.

'Whatever we need to,' Elsie said firmly.

They stayed in Elsie's room that night. The corpse that had been their father, they locked in the other room. He was nothing to them, nothing at all

They woke to hear the letterbox clang. An invitation to the Festival of Masks was on the doormat. A chance for a new life.

Elsie found a payphone and dialled the number. There was no interview. Geoff told her to make her way to Hudderford. You were born to be the Hare, he had proclaimed. With a huge smile, she had used the last of their money, supplemented by her late father's purloined wallet, to book the coach immediately.

This was their chance for a new life.

Chapter Ten

2nd May, 2013, Hudderford, Kent

E lsie leapt forwards, her lips drawn back across her bared teeth in a feral snarl. Geoff raised his truncheon but was forced back in to the chair. He tried to barrel forwards into her, screaming 'Once more unto the brea—' She brought her truncheon down onto Geoff's balding head. Crunch, it smacked into the egg-shaped skull. His jowls wobbled as his eyes rolled back into his skull. He even managed to make falling unconscious a theatrical experience.

She looked at the collapsed thespian and sneered.

Beside him on a small table were four envelopes with names written in elaborate calligraphy. Elsie shuddered at the sight of them but slid them into her pocket before running behind the bar. Grabbing the crossbow, she used the crank to pull the string back and loaded it with a quarrel.

Footsteps echoed. 'Geoff!' she recognised the voice from earlier. It was the man who had been berated for leaving his post. Slinking back beside the door, she waited as he and his partner entered.

Thunk.

A crossbow bolt erupted from the throat of the errant guard as blood blossomed from the wound. He turned to face her. He looked more offended than angry as he scrabbled at the open wound with grasping fingers.

His partner charged her. Elsie threw the crossbow into his face and kicked over a stool into his path. He stumbled and overextended his truncheon. Her first strike broke his wrist. The follow-up strike hit his jaw. Blood and teeth exploded from his face as he fell to the floor, his hands cradling his head. She didn't pause. Every place on his skull she saw exposed was struck. Again and again. Bone, brain matter and gore covered her, and she lashed until, out of breath, she straightened up. His partner took his last gasp, an expression of horror on his face, frozen like a mask.

Running upstairs, she shook Faith awake. She was still drowsy, but luckily hadn't undressed when Elsie put her to bed earlier.

'We're in danger, Faith. We don't have time to talk. We have to run.'

Faith blinked sleepily . 'Wha—'

'—Get up.' She pulled her sister up. Faith trusted her implicitly. With all that their family had been through, she had to.

Grabbing their bag, Elsie paused briefly. Seeing the framed photo of her mother in happier times, she pushed it safely in the bag and led Faith downstairs.

Faith gasped at the sight of the bodies.

Elsie strode into the kitchen, dragging Faith behind her. She turned on all the cooker gas taps. Then she shook her head.

It won't be enough.

Elsie reached around the cooker to unscrew the main gas valve as well. It hissed venomously.

A tray of candles for the tables was on one side. The small green glass holders were in the shape of apples. She lit several of them with a gaslighter until she heard noises outside. It would have to do.

Other people, no, not people, hounds, were approaching The Apple and Pear.

'Come on,' she whispered urgently, dragging Faith outside to the car park.

She heard the cries as the bodies were found and jogged faster. 'Come on, Faith!' Her sister, still suffering from the effect of the drugs, stumbled along beside her. She clung to Elsie's arm like a lead weight.

It's three miles to the town.

They'd never make it.

The thought had barely crossed her mind when a heavy weight landed on her back and she was rolled to the ground. The grinning face of Geoff looked down at her. His face was a crimson mask of drying gore. He punched her full in the face. The wooden mask broke her nose under the impact. Then his hands were clutching her throat, squeezing with manic energy. His mouth foamed with crimson spittle as he grunted with the effort. He pulled her up by the neck and smashed her head down onto the car park gravel again and again. She tried to loosen his grip, but he was too strong. Blood gushed from her nose down into her open mouth as she gasped for air. All she could taste was the coppery tang of her own bleeding wounds.

'I don't think so, my little starlet. The show *must* go on.'

Behind Geoff, the world exploded into fire and flame. The wind was knocked out of their lungs. All they could hear was the blast. Geoff's grip relaxed as it hit him and he was propelled forwards. He turned to look at the broken shell of the pub with shock. Flames licked from the surrounding hellscape. Smoke and ash littered the sky.

Elsie's hand scooped up a fistful of gravel. She ground it into Geoff's eyes. He howled and rubbed at them as she tried to wriggle out from under him. His dead weight was too much.

Instead, she grabbed his waistcoat, pulling him forward and pivoting. He crashed down onto the floor next to her and she was able to roll away.

Faith ran in and kicked at his body as he struggled to stand.

His breath was ragged and his voice raspy. He looked at Elsie with pure hatred, ignoring her tiny sister. 'It's the final curtain call for you.' He shoved Faith, who fell to the ground with a squeal.

With her ears still ringing, Elsie heard none of his final words. 'Oh, just fucking die,' Elsie growled as she pulled the truncheon out from under her hoody.

At the last minute, he cleared enough of the grit from his eyes to see the avenging angel bearing down on him. 'No, wait, ple—'

She never heard the rest. This time, she made sure he was dead. She raised the truncheon. His body shuddered under her relentless assault.

She reached into his pockets and pulled out his car keys.

She staggered around the car park. Tinnitus deafened her as she hammered the buttons on the car keys. Only hope and desperation kept her going.

Her mask restricted her vision.

Luckily, Geoff's Land Rover was easy to spot with its blinking lights. It loomed over the other vehicles. Racing forwards, Elsie looked at the shattered glass. The back seats were covered in sharp shards, but the front windows seemed to be intact. Pulling her hoody off over the mask, she quickly wiped as much of the glass off the front seats as she could and the two girls clambered in. The engine roared as they drove out down the lane.

The journey seemed a blur. Elsie could barely recall the elements of it. She parked outside the coach station and stumbled towards the first coach she saw idling.

The driver laughed. 'Jesus, I can't party like that these days. A whiff of lager and I get a three-day hangover.' He motioned behind him. 'Go sleep it off. If you feel sick, use the toilet.' He shook his head. 'Kids these days. What did you get up to?'

'You don't want to know,' Elsie muttered. Reaching into her pocket, she pulled out the envelope and took out a twenty. From the driver's expression, it was obvious what he thought of a girl in a bunny mask carrying an envelope of cash.

Better that than the truth.

'Just be sure to use the toilet if you feel ill,' he warned.

'Don't worry about us. We haven't been drinking,' Elsie meekly said. She crawled to the back of the coach. Faith worked on the leather straps of the mask with her pocket knife until the hateful thing came free. With a gasp of relief, Elsie felt the fresh air on her face as she tossed it to one side.

After a while, it was impossible to tell for how long, the coach driver yelled, 'All aboard for Newcastle.' The coach set off.

Hugging Faith, she felt she never wanted to let her go. Deep, wrenching sobs exploded from inside her as she realised they were free. The coach wound round the roads until it hit the first motorway. They leant against each other and slumbered as the rhythmic vibrations lulled them both to sleep.

Six hours later, the coach pulled into Newcastle coach station and the whole surreal episode continued when they were greeted by a nun.

'Elsie and Faith Peters?' she asked.

Elsie looked at the nun. She had nut-brown eyes and a warm smile, though it was ruined by a scar on her face which led from one side of her mouth up to her cheek.

'No, I don't know those names,' Elsie muttered.

The nun tutted. 'You shouldn't fib to a nun. Did you know the police are looking for you?' Elsie looked left and right. Her heart was pounding. 'Why don't you come and stay with us for a bit? We've been expecting you.'

'Who are you?' Elsie muttered.

'A nun. This isn't fancy dress. I'm from the Order of Saint Maria Goretti. We were all like you at one time before the order found us. Now we help others. My name is Sister Margaret.' She proffered a hand.

Elsie bit her lip. 'What if we don't want to come with you?'

'Then don't. No threats, no bribes. This is purely an offer of sanctuary with like-minded people.' Sister Margaret continued to hold out her hand.

Elsie looked down at it. 'Criminals, you mean?'

'Our only judge is St. Peter and of course, God Almighty. In their eyes, you are not a criminal. You are a victim. A victim who could save others from the same fate.' She smiled. 'You can leave at any time.'

'Elsie, come on.' Faith looked up at her, eyes pleading.

Elsie looked at Faith. She was too young to be on the run. A decision was made. She took the nun's hand. 'I'm not religious, though.'

Sister Margaret led her to a car where an elderly nun was waiting in the driver's seat. 'Neither was I. Then life happened. Maybe it will to you, maybe it won't.'

Thank You

Thank you for reading. I hope you enjoyed my story.

Please feel free to review my story on Amazon or Goodreads. Reviews are the single most useful thing for any author. We rely on them both for sales and more importantly, to get feedback to hone our craft.

Newton Webb

Acknowledgments

To my mother, Gillian Mary Webb, you gave me the two greatest gifts I could ever ask for.

As an author, you inspired me to write and as a librarian, you empowered me to read.

About The Author

Newton Webb was born in RAF Halton, England, in 1982. He has worked as a computer programmer and a table top games designer, but now writes full time.

He has a pet tortoise called Gill and a pet venus fly trap called Frank.

Join Newton Webb Online

'The World of Newton Webb' Mailing List
Promising a new story every month to download as a free eBook and free audiobooks.
https://www.newtonwebb.com/mailinglist

Facebook
https://www.facebook.com/thenewtonwebb/

Instagram
https://www.instagram.com/newtonwebb_author/

Twitter
https://www.twitter.com/thewebb

Free Audiobook: Festival of the Damned

Click HERE to download a FREE copy of the Festival of the Damned audiobook, narrated by Newton Webb.
Or use this link: https://www.buzzsprout.com/1958020/1102
9798

Free eBook: The Tattoo

Elsie's story continues in The Tattoo and The Wait, the short story sequels to Festival of the Damned.

The Tattoo
A stranded hitchhiker is picked up by a lorry driver. Spinning each other tales to pass the time they learn that neither is who they appear to be.

Get your free copy of The Tattoo HERE.
https://tinyurl.com/5ej7m8zf

Free eBook: The Wait

Elsie's story continues in The Tattoo and The Wait, the short story sequels to Festival of the Damned.

The Wait
A hapless romantic waits outside his girlfriend's office intending to apologise but instead gets drawn into an ever more deadly adventure.

Get your free copy of The Wait HERE.

https://www.newtonwebb.com/post/free-from-new-ton-webb-the-wait

Also By Newton Webb

Short stories and audiobooks by Newton Webb, available on Amazon Kindle Store

Amazon

Festival of The Damned

The Black Fog

Hunted

The Heir Apparent

The Platinum Service

Smoke in the Sewers

NewtonWebb.com

Home to a wide variety of the authors free short stories and audiobooks.

NewtonWebb.com

Made in the USA
Las Vegas, NV
05 October 2023

78575483R00046